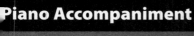
Piano Accompaniment

Alfred's
INSTRUMENTAL
PLAY-ALONG

Favorite HYMNS
INSTRUMENTAL SOLOS

TWINSBURG LIBRARY
TWINSBURG OHIO

WC
SM
Instrumental
Violin
Fav

Arranged by Bill Galliford, Ethan Neuburg and Tod Edmondson

 Alfred Cares. Contents printed on recycled paper.

No part of this book shall be reproduced, arranged, adapted, recorded, publicly performed, stored in a retrieval system, or transmitted by any means without written permission from the publisher. In order to comply with copyright laws, please apply for such written permission and/or license by contacting the publisher at alfred.com/permissions.

© 2010 Alfred Music Publishing Co., Inc.
All Rights Reserved. Printed in USA.

ISBN-10: 0-7390-7183-1
ISBN-13: 978-0-7390-7183-0

Photograph courtesy of Barry Erra

Alfred

Contents

AMAZING GRACE

TRADITIONAL AMERICAN MELODY

Amazing Grace - 5 - 1
36133

© 2010 ALFRED MUSIC PUBLISHING CO., INC.
All Rights Reserved

6

ALL CREATURES OF OUR GOD AND KING

By St. FRANCIS of ASSISI and
GEISTLICHE KIRCHENGESANGE, COLOGNE

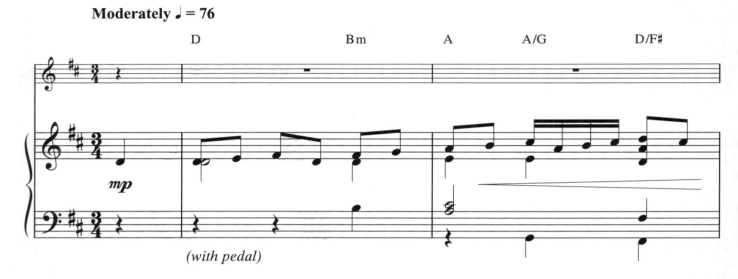

All Creatures of Our God and King - 4 - 1
36133

© 2010 ALFRED MUSIC PUBLISHING CO., INC.
All Rights Reserved

All Creatures of Our God and King - 4 - 4
36133

HOLY, HOLY, HOLY! LORD GOD ALMIGHTY

By JOHN B. DYKES
and REGINAL HEBER

Holy, Holy, Holy! Lord God Almighty - 3 - 1
36133

© 2010 ALFRED MUSIC PUBLISHING CO., INC.
All Rights Reserved

Holy, Holy, Holy! Lord God Almighty - 3 - 2
36133

JOYFUL, JOYFUL, WE ADORE THEE

By HENRY VAN DYKE
and LUDWIG VAN BEETHOVEN

Moderately, majestically ♩ = 108

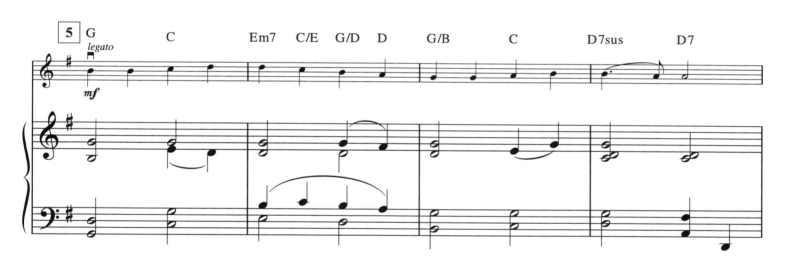

Joyful, Joyful, We Adore Thee - 3 - 1
36133

© 2010 ALFRED MUSIC PUBLISHING CO., INC.
All Rights Reserved

A MIGHTY FORTRESS IS OUR GOD

By MARTIN LUTHER

Majestically ♩ = 92

© 2010 ALFRED MUSIC PUBLISHING CO., INC.
All Rights Reserved

A Mighty Fortress Is Our God - 4 - 4
36133

BE THOU MY VISION

TRADITIONAL IRISH HYMN

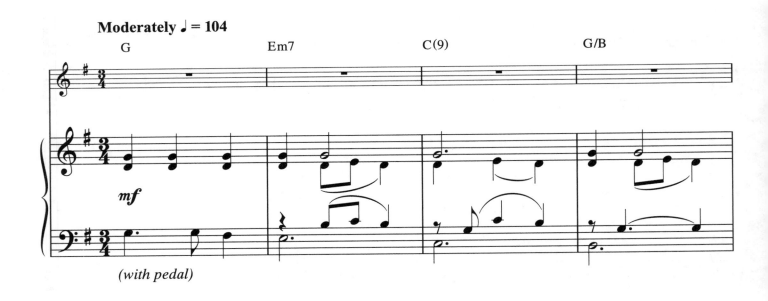

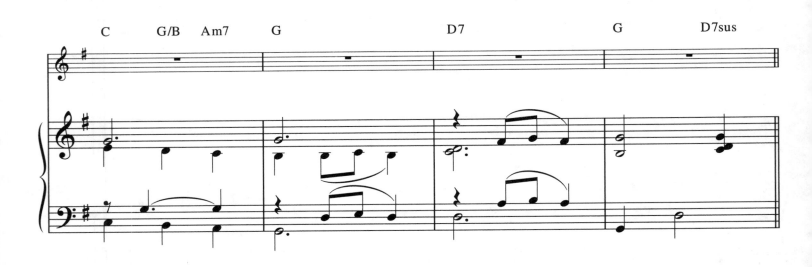

Be Thou My Vision - 4 - 1
36133

© 2010 ALFRED MUSIC PUBLISHING CO., INC.
All Rights Reserved

Be Thou My Vision - 4 - 4
36133

IT IS WELL WITH MY SOUL

By HORATIO G. SPAFFORD
and PHILIP P. BLISS

Moderate gospel feel ♩ = 104

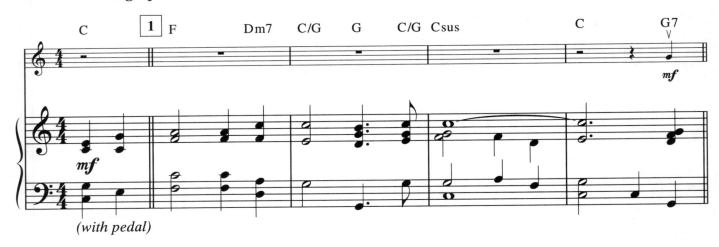

It Is Well With My Soul - 4 - 1
36133

© 2010 ALFRED MUSIC PUBLISHING CO., INC.
All Rights Reserved

28

It Is Well With My Soul - 4 - 3
36133

Alfred's
INSTRUMENTAL
PLAY-ALONG

Favorite HYMNS
INSTRUMENTAL SOLOS

Arranged by Bill Galliford, Ethan Neuburg and Tod Edmondson

♲ **Alfred Cares.** Contents printed on recycled paper.

© 2010 Alfred Music Publishing Co., Inc.
All Rights Reserved. Printed in USA.

No part of this book shall be reproduced, arranged, adapted, recorded, publicly performed, stored in a retrieval system,
or transmitted by any means without written permission from the publisher. In order to comply with copyright laws,
please apply for such written permission and/or license by contacting the publisher at alfred.com/permissions.

Alfred

ISBN-10: 0-7390-7183-1
ISBN-13: 978-0-7390-7183-0

Photograph courtesy of Barry Erra

Contents

Track 2: Demo
Track 3: Play Along

AMAZING GRACE

TRADITIONAL AMERICAN MELODY

© 2010 ALFRED MUSIC PUBLISHING CO., INC.
All Rights Reserved

ALL CREATURES OF OUR GOD AND KING

Track 4: Demo
Track 5: Play Along

By St. FRANCIS of ASSISI and
GEISTLICHE KIRCHENGESANGE, COLOGNE

© 2010 ALFRED MUSIC PUBLISHING CO., INC.
All Rights Reserved

HOLY, HOLY, HOLY! LORD GOD ALMIGHTY

Track 6: Demo
Track 7: Play Along

By JOHN B. DYKES
and REGINAL HEBER

© 2010 ALFRED MUSIC PUBLISHING CO., INC.
All Rights Reserved

JOYFUL, JOYFUL, WE ADORE THEE

Track 8: Demo
Track 9: Play Along

By HENRY VAN DYKE
and LUDWIG VAN BEETHOVEN

36133

© 2010 ALFRED MUSIC PUBLISHING CO., INC.
All Rights Reserved

A MIGHTY FORTRESS IS OUR GOD

Track 10: Demo
Track 11: Play Along

By MARTIN LUTHER

36133

© 2010 ALFRED MUSIC PUBLISHING CO., INC.
All Rights Reserved

Track 12: Demo
Track 13: Play Along

BE THOU MY VISION

TRADITIONAL IRISH HYMN

36133

© 2010 ALFRED MUSIC PUBLISHING CO., INC.
All Rights Reserved

IT IS WELL WITH MY SOUL

Track 14: Demo
Track 15: Play Along

By HORATIO G. SPAFFORD
and PHILIP P. BLISS

© 2010 ALFRED MUSIC PUBLISHING CO., INC.
All Rights Reserved

GREAT IS THY FAITHFULNESS

Track 16: Demo
Track 17: Play Along

Music by
WILLIAM M. RUNYAN

Great Is Thy Faithfulness - 2 - 1
36133

© 1923 (Renewed) HOPE PUBLISHING COMPANY, Carol Stream, IL 60188
This Arrangement © 2010 HOPE PUBLISHING COMPANY
All Rights Reserved   Used by Permission

HIS EYE IS ON THE SPARROW

Track 18: Demo
Track 19: Play Along

By CIVILLA D. MARTIN
and CHARLES H. GABRIEL

Gently, with expression (♩ = 108)

His Eye Is on the Sparrow - 2 - 1
36133

© 2010 ALFRED MUSIC PUBLISHING CO., INC.
All Rights Reserved

HOW GREAT THOU ART

Track 20: Demo
Track 21: Play Along

Words and Music by
STUART K. HINE

How Great Thou Art - 2 - 1
36133

© 1949, 1953 (Renewed) by THE STUART HINE TRUST
All Rights in the U.S. (excluding print rights) Administered by EMI CMG PUBLISHING
Exclusive U.S. Print Rights Administered by HOPE PUBLISHING COMPANY, Carol Stream, IL 60188
This Arrangement © 2010 THE STUART HINE TRUST
All Rights Reserved   Used by Permission

O THE DEEP, DEEP LOVE OF JESUS

Track 22: Demo
Track 23: Play Along

By SAMUEL TREVOR FRANCIS
and THOMAS J. WILLIAMS

Slowly and tenderly (♩. = 60)

O the Deep, Deep Love of Jesus - 2 - 1
36133

© 2010 ALFRED MUSIC PUBLISHING CO., INC.
All Rights Reserved

O the Deep, Deep Love of Jesus - 2 - 2
36133

'TIS SO SWEET TO TRUST IN JESUS

Track 24: Demo
Track 25: Play Along

By LOUISA M. R. STEAD
and WILLIAM J. KIRKPATRICK

Moderate folk style (♩ = 82)

36133

© 2010 ALFRED MUSIC PUBLISHING CO., INC.
All Rights Reserved

Favorite HYMNS
INSTRUMENTAL SOLOS

A Mighty Fortress Is Our God

All Creatures of Our God and King

Amazing Grace

Be Thou My Vision

Great Is Thy Faithfulness

His Eye Is on the Sparrow

Holy, Holy, Holy (Lord God Almighty)

How Great Thou Art

It Is Well With My Soul

Joyful, Joyful, We Adore Thee

O the Deep, Deep Love of Jesus

'Tis So Sweet to Trust in Jesus

This book is part of a string series arranged for Violin, Viola, and Cello. The arrangements are completely compatible with each other and can be played together or as solos. Each book features a specially designed piano accompaniment that can be easily played by a teacher or intermediate piano student, as well as a carefully crafted removable part, complete with bowings, articulations and keys well suited for the Level 2-3 player. A fully orchestrated accompaniment CD is also provided. The CD includes a DEMO track of each song, which features a live string performance, followed by a PLAY-ALONG track.

This book is also part of Alfred's Favorite Hymns Instrumental Solos series written for Flute, Clarinet, Alto Sax, Tenor Sax, Trumpet, Horn in F and Trombone. An orchestrated accompaniment CD is included. A **piano accompaniment** book (optional) is also available. Due to level considerations regarding keys and instrument ranges, the arrangements in the **wind instrument** series are not compatible with those in the **string instrument** series.

alfred.com

GREAT IS THY FAITHFULNESS

Music by
WILLIAM M. RUNYAN

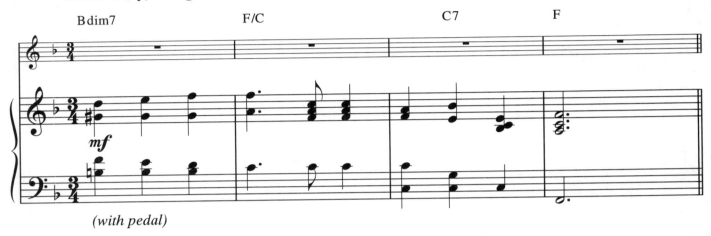

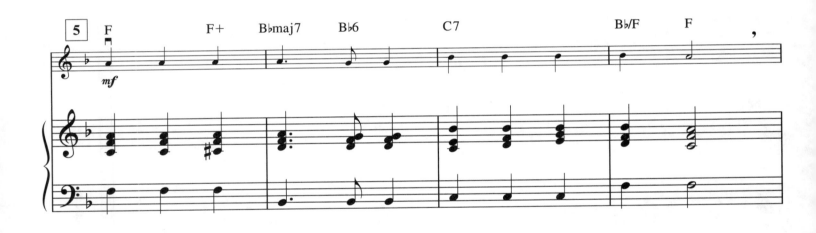

Great Is Thy Faithfulness - 5 - 1
36133

© 1923 (Renewed) HOPE PUBLISHING COMPANY, Carol Stream, IL 60188
This Arrangement © 2010 HOPE PUBLISHING COMPANY
All Rights Reserved   Used by Permission

32

Great Is Thy Faithfulness - 5 - 4
36133

34

Great Is Thy Faithfulness - 5 - 5
36133

HIS EYE IS ON THE SPARROW

By CIVILLA D. MARTIN
and CHARLES H. GABRIEL

His Eye Is on the Sparrow - 5 - 1
36133

© 2010 ALFRED MUSIC PUBLISHING CO., INC.
All Rights Reserved

His Eye Is on the Sparrow - 5 - 3
36133

38

His Eye Is on the Sparrow - 5 - 4
36133

HOW GREAT THOU ART

Words and Music by
STUART K. HINE

How Great Thou Art - 5 - 1
36133

© 1949, 1953 (Renewed) by THE STUART HINE TRUST
All Rights in the U.S. (excluding print rights) Administered by EMI CMG PUBLISHING
Exclusive U.S. Print Rights Administered by HOPE PUBLISHING COMPANY, Carol Stream, IL 60188
This Arrangement © 2010 THE STUART HINE TRUST
All Rights Reserved   Used by Permission

41

How Great Thou Art - 5 - 2
36133

42

How Great Thou Art - 5 - 4
36133

44

How Great Thou Art - 5 - 5
36133

O THE DEEP, DEEP LOVE OF JESUS

By SAMUEL TREVOR FRANCIS
and THOMAS J. WILLIAMS

O the Deep, Deep Love of Jesus - 5 - 1
36133

© 2010 ALFRED MUSIC PUBLISHING CO., INC.
All Rights Reserved

46

O the Deep, Deep Love of Jesus - 5 - 2
36133

48

O the Deep, Deep Love of Jesus - 5 - 4
36133

O the Deep, Deep Love of Jesus - 5 - 5
36133

'TIS SO SWEET TO TRUST IN JESUS

By LOUISA M. R. STEAD
and WILLIAM J. KIRKPATRICK

Moderate folk style (♩ = 82)

'Tis So Sweet to Trust in Jesus - 5 - 1
36133

© 2010 ALFRED MUSIC PUBLISHING CO., INC.
All Rights Reserved

52

53

'Tis So Sweet to Trust in Jesus - 5 - 4
36133

'Tis So Sweet to Trust in Jesus - 5 - 5
36133